ROCKET-L
A Spaceflight Lullaby

By Danna Smith
Illustrated by Ziyue Chen

A GOLDEN BOOK • NEW YORK

Educators and librarians, for a variety of teaching tools, visit us at
RHTeachersLibrarians.com
Library of Congress Control Number: 2017947060
ISBN 978-1-5247-6894-2 (trade) — ISBN 978-1-5247-6895-9 (ebook)
Printed in the United States of America
10 9 8 7 6 5 4 3 2

Rocket-bye, Baby, up to the moon.
Nighttime is falling; sleep will come soon.
We'll climb in the spaceship
    and that's where we'll stay,
snuggled up close as we're carried away.

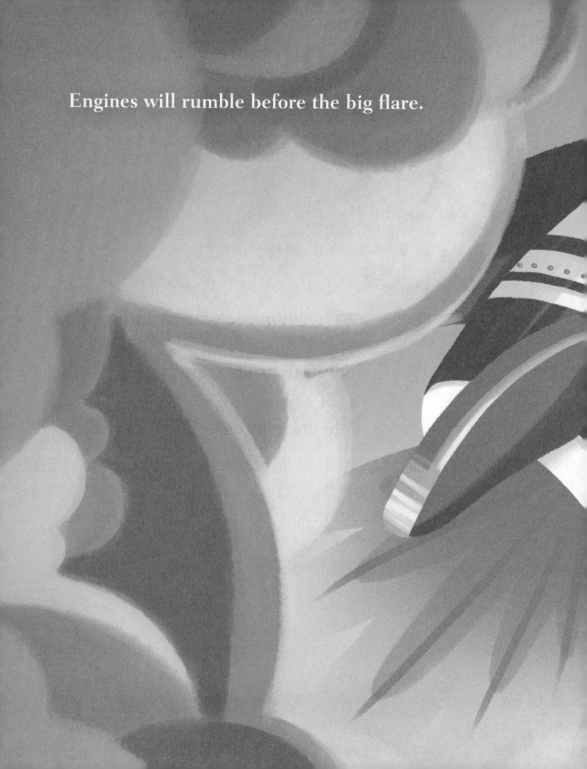

Engines will rumble before the big flare.

Then we'll lift off
and soar through the air.

Up and away through pillows of white . . .

over the edge of Earth on our flight.

Way up in space, you'll float from your bed—
ten tiny toes up over your head.

We'll stargaze together and then make a wish
upon a big bear, a lion, a fish.

Watching in awe as meteors race,
we'll pass other babies sailing
through space.

The moon, big and bright,
    will wink when she spies . . .
YOU, my dear baby,
    rubbing your eyes.

Sharing her moondust from craters so deep,
she'll blow you a kiss and send you to sleep.

On the way home,
we'll make our way through

blankets of stars to Earth,
round and blue.

Down we will glide through velvety black.

I love you, dear Baby—
to the moon and back.